Judith Humphries

The April Rebellion

Bumblebee Books
London

A CIP catalogue record for this title is
available from the British Library.

ISBN: 978-1-83934-052-9

Bumblebee Books is an imprint of
Olympia Publishers.

First Published in 2021

Bumblebee Books
Tallis House
2 Tallis Street
London
EC4Y 0AB

Printed in Great Britain

www.olympiapublishers.com

Dedication

For Luke and Jack, with love.

The Carter Family

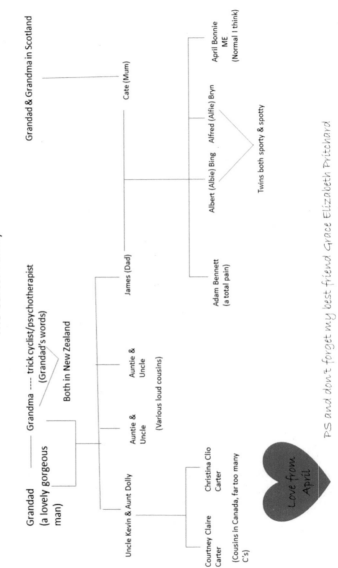

Grandad & Grandma in Scotland

Grandad ———— Grandma ---- trick cyclist/psychotherapist
(a lovely gorgeous   (Grandad's words)
man)
                         Both in **New Zealand**

Cate (Mum)

James (Dad)

Uncle Kevin & Aunt Dolly   Auntie &   Auntie &
                                Uncle   Uncle

Courtney Claire   Christina Clio   (Various loud cousins)
Carter   Carter

(Cousins in Canada, far too many
C's)

Adam Bennett
(a total pain)

Albert (Albie) Bing   Alfred (Alfie) Bryn

Twins both sporty & spotty

April Bonnie
ME
(Normal I think)

Love from
April

PS and don't forget my best friend Grace Elizabeth Pritchard

My family and me

My name is April. I hate my name. My birthday is April 1st and my oldest brother always calls me "The Fool" or "TF" when he thinks he is funny — which he isn't, ever.

My oldest brother is called Adam, he is sixteen years old and has a girlfriend. They kiss when they think no-one is looking. I don't think Mum would be too pleased about what they get up to when they know nobody is looking. He is called Adam because he was Mum and Dad's first boy, their first-born male child. Pathetic. I bet they thought they were really clever and that no-one had ever thought of that before. Honestly.

Then there are the twins. They are thirteen and both boys — Alfie and Albie — Alfred and Albert. Albert is Albert after Queen Victoria's husband who brought the Christmas Tree into this country. Apparently, Mum went into labour when she overstretched and toppled over when putting the fairy on the Christmas tree. For a bit it was all very worrying, but the twins were none the worse for an unexpected fall into tinsel and plastic toys. As for Alfie, he is Alfred, and of course Mum, in the advanced state of pregnancy forgetfulness, burned the Christmas cake. They are identical twins, born very close together, and I have no idea who came first and neither do they most likely.

Then comes me, April (yuck) — I am ten and will always be the youngest and smallest, and most put upon.

For heaven's sake, four kids all with names that start with 'A'. What about individuality? What about difference and independence? What about acknowledging from the very beginning that your kids were individual beings and deserved respect?

But this name malarkey gets worse. We all have middle names that start with 'B' and then our surname is Carter. ABC — it's gruesome!

Adam is Adam Bennett — Mum was having a Jane Austen phase around the time of his birth. Albie is Albie Bing, excruciatingly continuing the Christmas theme — White Christmas and Bing Crosby (please keep up). Alfie is Alfie Bryn, as Dad is Welsh, and I am April Bonnie, after Bonnie Tyler. I did say that Dad was Welsh. He is a huge Bonnie Tyler fan and when he is particularly riled or annoyed by one of us or all of us collectively, he threatens that he will be getting "Lost in France" unless we stop. It took years before we realised the connection, so now the boys, who are learning French, suggest that that is a good idea and please do it as soon as possible. ("C'est une bonne idée, Papa" etc, etc…) Which, of course, he doesn't understand as he only speaks English — and Welsh, of course.

Mum and Dad are Cate (with a C like the actress who played Galadriel in Lord of the Rings) and not a K as she so embarrassingly reminds everyone at every opportunity. Formally she is Catherine — with a C etc, etc. Dad is James and certainly not Jim. It's not that he dislikes the name Jim, but Jim Carter is a famous actor and James Carter fills in forms all day at the council offices. He has just always been James — or Dad.

(Do you think Galadriel's mum and dad had problems naming her? Did they have a daft system too, but in Elvish, after all, Galadriel is a bit of a mouthful?)

As Grandad says we are the ABCs. It is just so embarrassing — especially when you think of the pleasure thinking up this name sequence gave Mum and Dad. I wish they hadn't bothered.

The final member of our family is the dog — Potts. He is a Heinz 57, a mongrel, a mixed breed or whatever dogs of unknown parentage are called these days, and he is gorgeous. Dad wanted to continue the ABC theme and call him Aneurin Bevan, Noory for short, who was a politician years ago I was told. Not surprisingly there were objections all round — even surprisingly from Mum. He became Potts Puppy and is now Potts the Dog and I would say his character and personality have benefitted hugely from not being given a name from a pointless formula.

There are other family members who will pop in and out of my story. Grandad (Dad's dad) lives nearby. He is alone as Grandma left him for her psychotherapist some years ago. She was having problems apparently. She is in New Zealand with the "trick cyclist" as Grandad called the psychotherapist and contact is limited. Dad doesn't talk about her too much but when he does, he usually gets sad and Mum is nice to him for a bit. It's easier if he gets sad around Easter, because he loves Marks and Spencer's Luxury Hot Cross Buns filled with butter and cheddar cheese, and these cheer him up no end. Actually, hot cross buns are usually available shortly after Christmas so Mum gets a stock in and freezes them just in case. Mum's mum and dad run a bed and breakfast in Scotland and we see them now and again and go up for holidays. On the way north, Dad always jokes that we might get "mate's rates" in their B and B, which is daft because, as far as I am aware, they don't charge us anything at all. Or is "Mate's Rates" another Bonnie Tyler song?

So that is us — the Carter family — all six of us (eight if you include Grandad and Potts the dog). Why am I telling you all this? What is my story?

I will tell you. My story is all about being the only girl after three boisterous active sporty (and spotty) boys, whose mum expects her to be quiet, gentle, and enjoy wearing PINK. Whose mum expects her to enjoy knitting, and sewing, and cooking, and shopping for pretty things — usually PINK and SPARKLY? Who has always bought her daughter dolls, and toys, and plastic nonsenses usually in various shades of PINK? Who has always decorated her only daughter's bedroom with themed wallpaper — usually fairy tales, TV programmes or flowers. Yuck — Yuck. Yuck.

This is the story of my REBELLION.

The Rebellion — a long slow process

Don't get me wrong, I like being a girl. I have no wish to be a boy and be more like my sporty (and spotty) brothers. I fully expect that when I am older, I will have children and may even be married to the father of those children — but then again, I may not.

But I do envy my brothers' active lives and the fact that they can choose what they want to do. For example, the twins were Cubs and then Scouts. I asked if I could be a Brownie when I was six, but I can remember my mum's shudder when I suggested it and her rationalisation in which she hoped that I would be more independent in my thinking rather than going along with group thinking — and anyway I did not suit brown and yellow. I suspect it was the colour scheme that, for Mum, was the most annoying feature of the Brownie organisation.

Her alternative group activity for me was ballet where any development would be physical and feminine and dainty. She signed me up immediately for lessons. I remember my pink shoes, pink tights, pink leotard, and pink sparkly wool bolero — all kept in a pink plastic rucksack with a design of pink-winged fairies. My hair was held in place — a bun at the back — with a bobble. Yes — it was pink.

Ballet didn't last. It just did not suit. It was not that I was too tall or too heavy, but I couldn't put in the gentle grace that ballet requires — and there was always a frown on my face. I knew that I couldn't stamp in fury and refuse to go — but just wait until I am a teenager and can stamp in fury etc, etc. If I did object, Mum pleaded and was cross and upset all at the same time, then she would drag me along to the ballet school and tell me to enjoy it. Drat!

Oh, how I wish I was bigger and stronger, and able to say 'No' and have it heard!

Don't get me wrong — again. I don't hate my mum. I have never hated her but it was so tiring and wearing and frustrating not being heard, and I suppose I don't make too much fuss because I hate upset. The three older sporty and spotty brothers cause enough noise and upset for ten families. I suppose I now want my own noise space. I do try to understand her behaviour; even at an early age I could understand that she was fighting a losing battle with her three sons who were growing up too fast and were already beyond her influence. I think she saw the boys as being Dad's responsibility and, of course, he let them get away with all sorts. Her attempts to get them to eat sensibly failed by and large — mind you, they do eat sensibly but they also eat rubbish (her word) and all to excess, which fuels their endless energy. They never stop — constant motion. And of course, there were three of them whereas there is only one of me.

So, when I came along, I reckon she could fulfil her PINK, gentle, non-sporty, careful-eating ambitions through this long-awaited daughter.

MY rebellion therefore has to progress bit by bit — perhaps even two steps forward and three steps back. Independence will be achieved slowly but surely over a long time and I will be patient — if I can. Some of the rebellion will be in the shape of sneaky underhand acts, but I can deal with the impact of that should she find out and disapprove — at least I hope I can. It will be a war where I wear her down bit by bit. Small changes will take place that become normal behaviour before she realises that she does not approve — and then it is all too late to undo the changes. I have to do all this alone, all by myself. The three brothers would be interested and supportive, and then they would be mean and tell her my plans. They would then get great delight in her stopping me doing whatever I had planned. As I said earlier, I will always be the youngest and smallest and most put upon, and also the least regarded in the family (I will show them — the rotters.)

As for Dad, he would say "I should ask your mother first". Hopeless.

You might be thinking that this is all very deep and ambitious for a ten-year old. Well, I have always read, and I have always thought, and I am good with words. I read my teacher's last report and "articulate" and "independent thinker" were some of the words she used. I read early and have always enjoyed the mysteries of other people's lives, even if those lives were made up. Reading was also my way of getting away from the constant racket created by the three boys. I would just disappear up to my (pink) bedroom and read under the bed with a torch — as far away as possible from the pinkness.

Of course, Mum influenced my reading and still does — I have whole sets of story books about ponies and fairies and puppies (all neatly arranged in order in MY room by Mum), and they are okay but you get fed up after a while. Number fifteen after fourteen with the same plot and outcome is usually a pain.

So, there we have the first act of rebellion. I have decided that I too want to create a racket, but initially it will be a small racket — and one all of my own. I will join the local library and somehow borrow books that are MY choice and mine alone. There are books out there that will fuel the imagination and not just keep me busy and away from the constant noise and activity of home. It is a small beginning but it is a start — and the only way is forward. Oh, keep your fingers crossed please.

But I need an ally I can rely on. My best pal Gracie. She won't let me down.

Gracie

Grace Elizabeth Pritchard — Gracie — is my best friend and will be forever. She lives at the other side of town so we only see each other at school unless the mums arrange playdates. (Please can we think of another name for an arranged activity at a child's home for children who left nursery years ago?) She was called Grace Elizabeth because her mum and dad liked the names — bliss. There were no themes or plans in her choice of names — even more bliss.

She has no brothers or sisters. Before Gracie came along there were a few babies who didn't live more than a few days or came too early. Gracie says her mum gets sad when they talk about the brothers and sisters that she might have had, and I have thought of suggesting Marks and Spencer's Luxury Hot Cross Buns but somehow it never seems right. Her mum has an illness that means she can't walk very far and she gets tired very quickly so she spends a lot of time in her bedroom asleep. Her dad has an important job and works away a lot so they have a live-in housekeeper/nanny/nurse. Their house is the opposite of ours — it is quiet and peaceful and, as it is bigger, it has so much more space to do things in — to do things in private rather than under the bed away from the pink and chaos.

Grace has a huge bedroom and she decided how it should be decorated. Her choice was a bit too pink for me but there are posters and pictures and all sorts scattered about. But I wonder if it is because she can't walk far that means that Gracie's mum doesn't come into her room too often — and more importantly she doesn't change things around and add things, and generally interfere.

But oddly, Gracie loves coming to our house. It is so unlike her own; cramped and messy and noisy, and full of people. Gracie loves the racket created by my brothers and looks on in envy as they play football or mess in the garden. Of course, if she asked them if she could join in, they would tell her to "Shove off" — or another "off" which makes Mum and Dad really cross. Gracie wants to be part of other people's racket whereas I want my own racket. She even loves reading under my bed — it is our small private den she says.

I really love the peace and quiet of Gracie's house. I love having a choice of rooms where I can read and play, and Gracie has every toy in every colour you could ever want, which she is always happy to share. This clearly bothers my mum and dad who reckon she is spoilt because she has so many toys — bliss again. I overheard their conversation about Gracie's toys one day when I was hiding from Adam under the kitchen table. Adam was being was particularly obnoxious and I couldn't escape until Mum and Dad had moved to another room. I also heard a few other things that I didn't need to know.

But Gracie does have a lot of things — even her own mobile phone. She says I can have her old one when she gets a better one for her birthday. Being able to keep

Gracie's phone could be another part of the rebellion plan. My mum says I can have a mobile phone when I go to senior school with my brothers. That is nearly two years away — a whole two years, ages. By then, when I will be twelve, I will travel to school on my own but she will want to keep in touch, and she says I must ring up when I get to school so she can be sure I am there safely. And no, I can't join Facebook or any other things that are available on magic mobiles. Are all mums like this?

Whatever Mum and Dad think, to me Gracie is 100% perfect — 1,000,000% perfect. She is the best pal anyone could ever want. I explained my problem to her, most of which she already knew from previous chats. I also put my plan to her — we called the plan the "The April Rebellion" — and she agreed to help. We thought of sharing it with her mum — Gracie was sure she would understand but I thought no, at least not yet. The thought of Gracie's mum telling my mum was scary.

Am I doing the right thing? Sharing my thoughts and plans with Gracie felt like a betrayal of my own mum, who I know loves me to bits, and this all makes me so unsure of what I am doing. Am I the spoilt, selfish child that my mum and dad think Gracie is? After all, I have a happy, if always thoroughly annoying, family who are always there and always healthy, apart from the usual coughs and colds. What have I got to complain about? Surely as I got older, I would have more freedoms? Am I being impatient? Am I really just jealous of Gracie and her toys and books and private space? Am I jealous of Gracie having a mum who is ill? Am I being mean dragging Gracie into something that might end up making things worse for both of us? What an awful thought! What a mess.

Despite many doubts, we decided that the plan would go ahead, but there would be nothing in the plan that would or could deliberately hurt Mum (and Dad). I cannot exclude Dad because if the plans lead to trouble for me, he will be involved. Small steps, that might be nothing to others but would mean a lot to me, are the way forward. Oh heck. I wish I was eighteen and all this indecision had gone and my life was sorted.

The next step we decided was to make a plan of action — a list of things to do!

The plan(s) of action (not necessarily in order, apart from the library)

Joining the library

Asking for an allowance — not pocket money!

Mobile telephone earlier than 12th birthday

Clothes that are not a] pink and not b] picked entirely by Mum

Outside activities picked by me

Food choices

Having a laptop/computer

General unsupervised freedom – Unlikely but worth a try

Not fitting in with three brothers all the time

Making a fuss rather than avoiding fuss

Getting Dad onside

Getting Grandad onside

School uniform and wearing trousers generally

Gracie and I agreed that this all had to be done carefully and slowly, and one plan at a time. We agreed the library was a good first choice. Mum would have to be fully involved and we could then work out her mood for other plans — possibly. Gracie said she would join the library too, and perhaps we could go together with my mum as her mum didn't go out much, and Gracie said I could tell my mum that her mum would think this a good idea. Hmm — perhaps, after hearing Mum and Dad's conversation about Gracie, I was not sure that this was such a good idea. And this led to more bad feelings. Is this what growing up is all about — every new idea that is not a grown-up idea leads somehow to guilt and feeling awkward — even with your best pal?

First of all, it would just be me and Mum. Oh heck.

Joining the library

"Mum, may we go to the library on Saturday. I think I'd like to join" I said hopefully.

"The library — why on earth do you want to go there? You have plenty of books," Mum said, immediately dashing my hopes.

"Well the teachers at school keep mentioning it (not entirely true) and I thought I'd like to have a look first." — Me again.

"Hmm. I'm not too sure this is a good idea as the books might be old and dirty and we don't know where they've been. Your own books are always nice and new." — Mum.

"I'm sure that the people there take care of the books. Let's at least go and look. Please Mum. It would help me at school too." — Me again.

And so, it went on until there was a reluctant

"OK, but only for half an hour as I thought you might like Scottish Country Dancing and there is a class at midday."

Phew, Mum hadn't said 'No' — three steps forward and two back.

Our town library is a big, old brick building filled with rooms made of dark brown wood and glass with a pattern in it. The shelves are all dark brown wood and as we went in, I could hear my mum 'tut'. She likes white stuff — which is daft really as my three brothers make everything filthy and their mess wouldn't be seen if we had a dark brown house.

But I loved it immediately. The junior library was an Aladdin's Cave filled with all sorts of gorgeous, magical books and magazines. I rushed around looking at some books, and then rushed to other shelves, and then went back — back and forth, to and fro. My mum went to authors she knew and tried to get me to look at them, and I did for a bit, but then it was easy to just scamper off to another set of shelves. I had the best time — the loveliest time ever, ever, ever.

I picked four books and took them to the lady on the desk. Mum had to be part of this bit as we joined and filled in forms, and I could see that she didn't approve of two of the books I had picked. I had sneakily picked two that I knew she would approve of, and one of the others was actually a boy's adventure book. But the marvellous lady behind the counter said they were a good mixture and if I liked, she could help me choose some next time.

I said "Yes please" and "that would be lovely" — as Mum bristled and her lips seemed to be stuck firmly together.

One of my books was called *War Horse*, about horses in the First World War. Mum didn't like the title at all, but I explained we were doing the First World War at school in a project and it would be really helpful. I wonder if Mr Morpurgo has written anything else I might enjoy.

"Oh, all right then," she said — with lips tightly

together again. (Are these pursed lips? I'm not sure because what lips have to do with purses.)

I skipped down the library steps and jumped up and gave Mum a big kiss which surprised her. I think she was pleased though, and afterwards Scottish Country Dancing wasn't too bad. I didn't have to be dainty, and it was so energetic and confusing with all sorts of tricky patterns I got wrong time and time again. I kept bumping into the other dancers, but they didn't mind and just laughed.

Could this be the pattern for Saturdays — the library followed by Scottish Country Dancing?

I suggested this to Mum — that it might be a good idea to do both if I was ready to get new books on Saturdays.

"Hmm," she said but she didn't say 'no'. Perhaps, she wished she had had that idea. I hope so.

We got home after a bit of shopping where I didn't argue too much when she bought me some white sparkly-tights — I would rather have had the navy blue sparkly-tights but that would have been pushing my luck. (Actually, I would have much preferred a pair of tight jeans that just reached my ankles — Gracie has some, of course, and they are gorgeous — but that was asking too much especially after the first plan had gone so well.)

I had to tell Dad and the boys when I got home. The boys were just not interested and wouldn't even look at my library books, but Adam's girlfriend Aimee was at home, and she had a look. She must have had an accident as there was a big bruise on her neck but she blushed when I asked what she had done. Baffling. And then Dad took Adam into the dining room for a private word. Even more baffling.

Anyway, most importantly, Aimee said she had lots of books at home she didn't want anymore, and she would fetch them over for me to look at and I could keep whatever ones I wanted.

Hoo hoo — the perfect day had just become even more perfect even though Mum's lips were tightly together again. But I said "Yes please," in my best and most enthusiastic voice and that was that.

Things to remember:

A: I must get to Aimee's books before Mum does and get them into my bedroom before she can check them out.

B: I must ask Aimee why her name has 2 'E's and not a 'Y'. One of the books I checked out at the library was *Little Women*, and there was an Amy in that and she was certainly not Aimee.

C: I must tell Gracie about the success of the first plan and that even Scottish Country Dancing wasn't too bad. She will be so pleased. If only I had her mobile phone now! I could use the landline but that is risky — Mum and even sporty, spotty brothers listen in.

I haven't mentioned Dad. When I told him about our day and showed him my books, he was so pleased for me. I think there were tears in his eyes and he gave me the biggest cuddle ever, and £1, and said "That's my best girl".

But I'm his only girl. Has he any secret daughters? I will ask Grandad. It would be so nice to have a sister or two.

Getting Grandad onside

I see Grandad on Sundays. Dad drops me off at me to Grandad's house and then takes the twins to football or whatever. Adam is less likely to take part in Sunday sports these days as he sleeps over at Aimee's house (not Amy's house) on Saturday night — another thing he had had private chats in the dining room with Dad about. It must be very embarrassing for him at Aimee's house if he needs to pee in the middle of the night as he doesn't take his pyjamas — I checked — pyjamas in use are under his pillow or on the floor, and washed pjs in the drawer. Of course, I do not wear pyjamas. I have nightdresses with pretty patterns on them — usually flowers. I recently found an accidental tear in a particularly gruesome nightie covered with kittens patting away balls of wool. This accidental tear somehow became bigger and less accidental. Needless to say, the replacement nightie had daisies on it despite a quiet comment to Mum that pyjamas would be nice for a change.

Anyway, on Sundays I go and spend time with Grandad while Mum cooks a huge traditional lunch that Grandad comes back with me for. If the weather is okay, we catch the bus and if it is rubbish, Dad collects us. It is a nice way to spend Sunday as Grandad watches recorded stuff on TV that Mum and Dad would never think okay. Don't get me wrong — it's not rude stuff just really daft stuff. Anyway, I thought I might tell Grandad at this next visit about my plan.

But it didn't work out as I planned. Grandad and I were watching an episode of 'Dad's Army' that Mum and Dad would have probably approved of, but I was miles away thinking about how to start our chat. Grandad must have noticed because I wasn't laughing at Private Pike — my favourite. He then said "What's on your mind Littley". Littley is his nickname for me and I like it — and I just burst into tears — huge sobs.

So, it all came out in between sobs and nose blows and hiccups. All about how I was not able to make any decisions about what I did — anything at all — and how my life was totally controlled by Mum, but I love Mum and I hate pink and I have a plan, but it is so scary having a plan.

He sat quietly for a while, gave me a big cuddle and switched off 'Dad's Army' — just as Captain Mainwaring said "Don't tell him, Pike". He then said he could see my difficulty but he was not in a position to interfere. Dad and Mum would be very cross if he got involved. He could see how I felt so hemmed in by Mum's decision-making but he could also see why Mum was hemming me in. After all, I was her last child, her last chance at being an active and busy mum, so Mum is probably holding on to me being dependent for as long as she can — especially as the boys are now beyond her. But he did say that if I needed to chat about the awfulness of it all I could come to him at any time. He also promised that he would tell nobody about our talk or my plan. He also said that things would probably get better as I got older, especially when I was at senior school. He didn't say just be patient, but him saying that it wouldn't last forever was helpful. I have had nightmares about me being ancient in my twenties and still being told what to do by my mother. Oh heck!

So, Grandad was on my side — sort of — but he couldn't really help.

We shared a Marks and Spencer's Luxury Hot Cross Bun — with butter and lemon curd — and got ready to go to my house for lunch. Luckily, it was a nice day so we were able to catch the bus and by the time I got home, my face was not red and blotchy with tears.

After lunch I went upstairs to my bedroom and started to read a new Jacqueline Wilson book under the bed with a torch — there have been two successful trips to the library so far — but I fell asleep almost straight away. Who would have thought rebellions could be so exhausting? When I woke up, Grandad was getting ready to go home and I think he gave me an extra big and tight hug before he left.

School uniform

At my school, the uniform for boys and girls is white-collared T-shirts with turquoise jumpers or cardigans, and the boys wear grey trousers or shorts, and the girls, grey trousers or skirts. I bet you can guess what Mum makes me wear — yes, skirts. I would love to wear trousers for school — they are easier to run in and the silly boys don't try to see the colour of your knickers (mine are always pink, or pink and white patterned). But Mum gets my uniform, and always when I am not there, and trousers never arrive. Gracie, of course, wears trousers all the time.

Gracie and I have a plan. I have some spare money and Gracie always has lots, so we went to the used uniform shop at school and bought 2 pairs of trousers that someone had grown out of. They were clean and ironed, and to my mind, gorgeous.

I took them home, sneaking them upstairs to my bedroom, and tried them on. They looked fabulous. I looked so tall and grown up — which I suppose Mum is trying to avoid for as long as possible. So, when would be the best time to present them with this alternative school-wear plan?

I figured the best time would be when the brothers (still sporty and spotty) were busy and when Mum and

Dad were together — perhaps on the sofa watching TV.

An evening came along when Adam was at Aimee's doing homework (fat chance) and the twins were at cricket practice. Mum and Dad were watching 'The One Show'. I put on the trousers, took a deep breath, and went downstairs and stood in front of them as they watched TV.

"Don't they look elegant?" I said, before Mum could say, "Take them off".

"My goodness," said Dad. "Where's my little girl?"

"Still here but wearing gorgeous, comfy and elegant trousers. What do you think?" I said — aiming my words at Dad.

"Lovely," he said. "They really suit you."

I could have cried and kissed him all at the same time. Then Mum spoke.

"They're not really appropriate for school," she said. "You are a girl and there is plenty of time for trousers when you are older."

"But Mum, all the girls wear trousers and I'm fed up being different and not able to join in some things because my legs are on show."

"She's right," said Dad (I owe him another kiss). "Skirts can be embarrassing for active girls — and our April is quite the athletic type." Mum of course did not like being told that I was athletic and not a dainty pink-wearer.

Well, this went on for ages but a compromise was reached. I think Dad being on my side helped — he would get hell from Mum, later on. I could wear trousers three days a week (better than nothing) until the end of term, and during the holidays, we would have another chat about it. Furthermore, she would buy new trousers for me — she was not impressed when I told her where my trousers had come from.

Well, I think that was a success. I danced back upstairs and couldn't wait to tell Gracie next day. I also owe her £4. I was thrilled.

Who knows, perhaps if the trousers are fully accepted, Mum might be persuaded to buy me pyjamas, (but do not rush things April — remember two steps forward and three steps back).

Next day, I was ready for school too late for Mum to tell me to get back into a skirt and wait until the new trousers had been bought. I hid under the bed for ten minutes and happily the twins were being pests and holding everything up, so she was ready to rush out when I came downstairs. (They might be twins but secretly I think they hate each other. This morning's fight was about football jerseys. A football jersey has been lost and they each blamed the other — pathetic!)

"Oh," she said — lips pursed, when she saw my covered legs.

"Come on Mum, we will be late," and I grabbed her hand and dragged her down the drive. There was silence and occasional frowns all the way to school where I saw Gracie waiting at the gate. I jumped up and gave Mum a quick kiss and said "Bye Mum — see you later," and dashed off before she could do a thing. I ran towards my best pal who had the biggest grin on her face when she saw my trousers.

I looked back and saw Mum walking away, perhaps

more slowly than usual. Despite feeling bad for her, I had the best day that was not even spoiled by double-maths. It was great looking down and not seeing knobbly knees. And of course, the trousers hid the hateful ankle socks with white frills. Bliss.

Perhaps the rebellion had better ease off for a bit. I have to be careful not to undo all that has been achieved so far and Mum must not get suspicious. Or perhaps I could do a bit of extra rebellion work on Dad for a while?

Honestly, I do love Mum and I can understand why she is as she is. Perhaps she should have had another little girl who might have appreciated the pinkness — and that would have taken the pressure off me.

Pocket money

A few weeks had gone by and nothing further had been said about the trousers or my reading choices, although there were a few more pursed lips than usual. Perhaps, Mum was starting to accept that I was still me even if I was making some decisions myself.

An opportunity rose to discuss pocket money one evening when she was out with her pal Eve, sharing a bottle of wine somewhere or other. Eve is Mum's equivalent of Gracie, and I bet Mum complains about me to Eve, as I do to Gracie about her. Eve is nice but is not married and has no children. She is a 'Career woman' (Mum's words) and is always flying off to interesting places with her job. Perhaps Mum is jealous of her? Eve wears gorgeous clothes with fancy labels and even looks good in pink. Amazing. Mum's clothes are usually from Marks and Spencer when she buys Luxury Hot Cross Buns.

Dad and I were watching 'University Challenge'. He tries so hard and, if he is lucky, he might get one question right in the whole half-hour programme. I enjoy watching it too, and trying to make sense of the questions is enough for me. These young people are so clever. I would like to be on 'University Challenge' one day.

"My name is April Carter and I am reading

Jacqueline Wilson books." And underneath the desk, I will be wearing trousers!

So, I said to Dad "As I'm getting older could I have an allowance instead of pocket money please?"

He looked baffled — but he said "Titian". He was wrong, the answer was 'Tintoretto'. Who are these people?

Then he said, "Aren't they the same?"

"Yes, but as I am older it would be nice to say that I am getting an allowance as small kids get pocket money, and I'm nearly eleven."

"Have you asked your mum?"

"No — (long pause) because you give out pocket money and not Mum — and it's just a name change. I'm not asking for more money — although that would be nice too."

"Blenheim Palace" he said — and then "Yes!" When Mr Paxman said that was the answer. He was very pleased with himself and this would have been a good time to ask for extra allowance but that would have been very sneaky.

"All right April, you now have a weekly allowance instead of pocket money which might be increased on your birthday if you are as old and mature as you seem to think you are." he said, frowning at a maths question from Mr Paxman.

"Thank you, and will you promise not to call it pocket money anymore — even if Mum does?"

"Okay — Cicero."

Cicero was right. Who are these people?

The boys get money from Dad too — I don't know

what they call it. Probably just money — I think over the years the 'pocket' bit has been lost, and Dad is always forking out for sporting stuff and Adam always needs money to treat Aimee. Now there's a thought — perhaps I might enjoy more organised sporty group stuff. That could be added to the 'Rebellion list'. I put up with Scottish Country dancing as it involves a trip to the library, but my other hobbies (hardly hobbies, they are things I do picked by Mum) are mostly solitary. (I had to look up how to spell solitary) — I have piano lessons (I am rubbish) and gymnastics (I told you I was athletic, and yes, my leotards are pink.)

I will have to think about that one. Mum will have a fit if I ask to play football.

The next thing is to have the freedom to spend the ALLOWANCE where and how I like. Usually I go shopping with Mum and yes, she tries to guide what I buy. I am too young to go out on my own — even with Gracie, so I can see that might be a problem. Actually, I don't think I would like to go shopping without Mum. I think it would be too scary. Perhaps I can do that when I am fourteen. Gracie goes out with the nanny/nurse/housekeeper occasionally, but she most often buys stuff from the internet — she does it lying in bed with her mum, who of course can't go out shopping. I am so jealous. But perhaps Gracie might let me buy stuff via her internet and with her mum alongside, of course? That would be a major rebellion — and might even cause a war.

Mum and Dad both have laptops, as have the boys as they use them for their school work. I hope when I'm in senior school, I will get a laptop too. Computers and stuff are not really what I have been interested in up to now, although I do have a tablet, discarded by Albie. It was packed with brutal games — yuck! Perhaps this has to change — I have to develop an interest in computer stuff if only to let me go shopping.

What I am finding is that each little act of rebellion leaves me with a lot of unexpected things to think about, and sometimes the changes, although usually wanted and lovely, almost always come with a few problems. For example, Mum is still not fully comfortable with me wearing trousers to school and when she sees what I am reading there is usually a "Tut" somewhere about. I have decided that when I have a daughter, I will let her choose what she wants to do — but obviously not all the time — and anything pink will definitely be off limits unless she asks very nicely.

This whole business is not as easy as I thought it might be.

P.S. Last Sunday I saw Grandad and reported my progress so far. He was pleased, and he loved my library books but then he said something very strange. He said, "Please don't grow up too quickly, Littley — you are only young once — enjoy it". And he looked a bit sad too.

Another thing to think about and worry about — oh dear.

A bit about Mum and Dad and others

I suppose I had better tell you a bit more about Mum and Dad or you'll be thinking she is a mean stinker and Dad is a gentle TV quiz addict.

Mum first. She has no brothers or sisters, or aunts and uncles, and therefore no cousins. She has no-one but us and her mum and dad, who run a B and B which is a bed and breakfast place where people come and stay overnight, usually on their holidays, in Scotland. We see them once a year. Her mum and dad seem to have spent their lives looking after other people — before the B and B they ran pubs, and before the pubs they had a hotel, and before that, when they had normal nine-to-five jobs, they fostered children from social services.

I overheard this hiding in the airing cupboard which is next to Mum and Dad's bedroom. Yes, I was hiding from Adam, but I had reason to — I had hidden his football boots. Mum thinks they had foster children live with them because her mum and dad wanted her to have friends. Their life was always moving from one place to another, and more often than not, as soon as Mum settled into school and started making friends, they were off again — to another new place.

But she didn't want friends — she just wanted her mum and dad to herself and to not share them with others.

In the pubs, they usually lived upstairs and her mum would put her to bed and be off very quickly as there were customers waiting to be served. The hotel was the worst as her mum and dad were busy all the time. At least in the pubs, they had the mornings to themselves.

She said to Dad that she thought her mum and dad were glad she got married early to him — at eighteen. They could then get on with looking after other people without having to bother with her. I think I heard tears at that point and Dad saying nice quiet things to her I couldn't make out.

It sounded all so sad and so unhappy. I know that we as a family have huge battles occasionally, but we are still happy and settled, and Mum and Dad love having us and being with us — something Mum never had.

Perhaps that is why she is like she is when she is with me. Perhaps she is trying to be a mum like she wanted her own mum to be — and never was. Having a mum who is too busy to properly bother must be awful. My mum bothers too much which is only occasionally awful and more of a nuisance than anything.

I feel really sorry for Mum. And I suppose my rebellion is also telling her that she is not wanted or needed, and that she is even in the way from time to time. Something is being repeated here and it is not pleasant for Mum.

But I can't arrange my life to make up for her miserable childhood. So, my feelings of guilt about the 'April Rebellion', that are never far away, have to be put to one side — but I will try not to hurt Mum.

As for Dad, he has a brother and two sisters — all

older, and I have lots of older cousins who are all completely bonkers. When they come to stay, I get tummy pains through laughing too much, and seeing Grandad so happy with all his family together, is the best thing.

But Dad's mum ran off with her psychotherapist (check spelling and is it the right word?) when Dad was eighteen, and she is now in New Zealand. We have seen her once in the last few years. Dad and Grandad were very sad when she left and Dad says Grandad has never really got over it all. He never bothered with another girlfriend and just concentrated on keeping his family together and happy. Which he did, and he is loved so much by everyone. As for Dad, he was nearly almost grown up and at university when she left, and he was already going out with Mum — and then she got pregnant and they got married before Adam arrived. Oops. I reckon that is why they keep having private chats with Adam in the dining room.

So, Dad went from one happy family to his own happy family and nothing seems to bother him too much.

As for my three brothers — I can't be bothered to explain how awful they always are — the rotters. They tease me, they ignore me, they don't let me play with them, they ignore Gracie (or tell her to shove off or worse), and when I am watching TV, they switch it over or even just off.

I really have to have a second rebellion organised against my brothers when this first one is sorted.

Perhaps that explains a bit why Mum is as she is — her own unhappy childhood and having three stinkers for sons.

Gracie's childhood is a bit like Mum's, in that she does not have a lot of time with her mum and dad. Her dad is away a lot and her mum is too ill. But Gracie, unlike my mum, knows her mum loves her heaps and heaps, as does her dad, and she knows that it is not her fault they have to have a nanny/nurse/housekeeper busy in the house instead of her mum. It just is what it is. But Gracie gets lots and lots of cuddles from her mum which I don't think my mum ever did. I get cuddles from both Mum and Dad — and I reckon I would get a few more if it wasn't for the three rotters.

And when I think of some of the others at school, everyone has something to be unhappy about. One girl in the year below mine, lives with her auntie as her mum and dad were killed in a plane crash. I can't think of anything more awful.

Now I'm feeling bad about the 'April Rebellion' again. Perhaps, I am just an ungrateful little girl.

Things that get in the way of my rebellion

This had better be in a list so I don't get in a muddle.

1. Mum is in Scotland looking after Grandad Scot and the B and B, as Grandma Scot is in hospital having a knee put right. Mum was not happy about this and I heard her say to Dad as he packed the car before taking her to the station.

"Why should I go? Why are they relying on me? They have never been there for me — ever. It's not right. It's not bloody fair."

Dad saw me looking and listening, and quickly said, "Shush, shush — you'll be back home in no time," and off she went.

To be fair she didn't say before she went stuff like she was relying on me to take care of the boys. That would have led to a huge extension to the rebellion. But she did say to my brothers that they were to "Muck in," and "don't expect Dad and April to run after you like I do." That was nice.

And we have managed OK. I agreed to do the washing up after breakfast and tea in return for a brief raise in the allowance as I knew the boys wouldn't even see the mess. There have been probably too many take-out pizzas and fish and chips, but Dad gets in late and he is too tired to cook, and the boys don't even know what a pan is.

There will be a lot of clothes washing for Mum when she gets back though. Dad has done the essentials but there is a lot of stuff lying about that needs a clean.

2. Adam and Aimee are finished and he is very unhappy (Do I care? — a bit perhaps). She told him they were spending too much time together and taking each other for granted, and she wants to work hard for her exams. They can meet as friends on Saturdays but no more than that, and no sleeping over. (I was under the dining room table during this private chat between Dad and Adam — I knew it was to take place as Adam asked for a dining room chat after tea, so I got there and hid before they arrived).

Dad was very good and kind and understanding, and Adam cried a bit — but I bet that, deep down, Dad is relieved. I bet he remembers what happened when he and Mum got too close when they were teenagers.

So, Adam is moping around and not catching up on school work or preparing for his exams. He really is hopeless.

3. The twins are even more awful than ever. They tease Adam rotten and sing, "Adam's been dropped — la la la la la la." Albie has a black eye as a result of this — there was a three-way fight that Adam won. Dad was not sympathetic — he said he deserved the punch and no, he wasn't going to let Albie have time off school. In fact, he was going to tell the school what happened and they were not to be sympathetic either.

I think we need a bigger house. The place would be a lot more peaceful if the twins had separate bedrooms —

ideally on different floors. I suggested this to Dad and he agreed, but a bigger house would be expensive and perhaps when Adam went to university, one of the twins could have his room.

"Fat chance of that happening," I said. "Adam does no work at all for school."

"Hmm." He replied.

"Perhaps I could go and live with Grandad?" I suggested. "No way," — he said. "Your mother would have a few fits." An interesting thought! "And I would miss you." Ah. I love my dad — so I gave him a cuddle.

4.   Horror   of   horrors   —   Gracie's nanny/nurse/housekeeper is leaving them — for six months at least, if not forever. Her name is Julia and she has decided she wants a bit of adventure in her life, and has handed in her notice and bought a rail ticket that will get her all over Europe. Gracie and her family are worried — Julia has held all the messy and practical bits of their family life together for ages. They are interviewing for someone who they hope will only be needed for a few months before Julia comes back, but according to Gracie, they are all like Miss Trunchbull in Roald Dahl's 'Matilda'.

I have discovered Roald Dahl at the library. My favourite book so far written by him, is 'Danny, Champion of the World'. That is what I will be one day — after I have appeared on 'University Challenge' of course.

What if Julia never comes back? What if she finds someone and falls in love, and gets married and has babies — all in 6 months? How will Gracie and her family cope?

5. Dad is thinking of converting our loft so there is room for Grandad to come to live with us. Grandad is finding it more and more difficult to do everything or

even anything well, and he is falling from time to time. He finds that so frustrating so, before he gets too bad, Dad has thought he might like to live with us. Even Mum thought it a good idea as Grandad would have been the sort of dad she never had. I said "Yes," immediately and that he can have my room, but Dad said "No." So that might be something to look forward to — while the rebellion continues.

It is impossible to carry on with my big rebellion while the rest of the world and my family have equally important things to do. Is that what being grown-up is all about — fitting things in and thinking about or doing things that have to be done rather than what you would choose to do? Is that what Grandad meant when he said I shouldn't grow up too quickly? Baffling.

Gracie is eleven

Gracie had her birthday recently and she became eleven-years old. She is a bit older than me but not much — a few months. Her party was really grown up for an eleven-year-old — we went to a bar where they served teatime 'mocktails' which are not proper cocktails. I know grown-ups have mocktails, cocktails that have no alcohol, but these were even less grown up than that — just interesting fruit juices with interesting bits of fruit floating on the top. They were gorgeous. And then we went to a sushi bar and had little rice and salmon things. I had never had sushi before and was surprised how much I liked it. And the boys have never had sushi at all — I think they were quite jealous of me.

But I had nothing to wear for what was a grown-up type of party. My clothes were too childish and when I asked Mum what she thought, she agreed that we would have to find something suitable. I was amazed but to be fair to Mum, she would not want me to be embarrassed and feel out of place at an event because I was wearing the wrong clothes. School uniform is different and that is why getting into trousers for school was tricky, but she understands that to look wrong at a swanky party would be so embarrassing.

So, we went shopping. I was dreading it as I thought

what she would like would be awful, but it wasn't too bad. We both chose a dress that was just like a long jumper in a nice light wool that came to above my knees. It was dark blue and yes, there was a bit of a pink pattern, but that amount of pink was okay. I wore it with pale-pink almost-white tights (lightweight, not heavy-duty wool tights) together with a pair of black ballet pumps I had in the wardrobe. I looked okay but felt fab — and appropriate. Mum looked pleased too but a bit sad — I really think she is sad that I am growing up. Mum found a little black shoulder bag and the outfit was complete.

I showed off my outfit to Dad and Grandad. Grandad also looked sad but pleased and proud, and Dad said I looked beautiful. He has never said that before — and Mum agreed. Amazing.

My present to Gracie was a book. She doesn't like stories but she loves reading poetry out loud. There is enough room in her house for her to read poetry out loud, very loud, and not upset anyone. So, I got her a book of poems you are supposed to learn 'off by heart' — whatever that means, and some posh hand cream. She was thrilled with her presents.

The party was brilliant but I could see that Mum — who dropped me off and collected me afterwards — was not happy and had pursed lips, when she saw some of the ten to eleven-year olds wearing make-up and with pierced ears. Thankfully, she didn't say anything but I could see she was not impressed. Meg (short for Margaret but she hates her full name) was beautifully made up because her mum works on the make-up counter at Boots and is good at that sort of thing, and Julie had three holes in each ear. I think make-up and pierced ears will have to be part of a second rebellion later on. I also reckon Dad would agree with Mum 100% on this too.

I have talked to Gracie about us getting our ears pierced and she is totally against it. She said she was not having any holes put anywhere on her body as her mum had had to have holes put in her body from time to time for medicines to go in, and sometimes they had got an infection which made her feel worse. Gracie was quite determined about all this. When she told me, she was sad and quiet for a bit. I hadn't realised just how ill Gracie's mum was, and I figured even a Marks and Spencer's Luxury Hot Cross Bun would not help.

Gracie's main present from her mum and dad was a new posh mobile phone and, as promised, she gave her old one to me. But it wasn't that simple. Her dad said there were things I needed to know and talk over with my mum and dad. First of all, I needed a sim card and a contract if they were happy for me to use it.

I had no idea mobile phones were so tricky. Do Mum and Dad pay for the boys' phones? Did they pay for Adam's almost constant phone calls and messages to Aimee until their recent break-up? Do they pay for the twins' games and stuff they are constantly playing?

This has to be done very carefully and at the right moment when Mum and Dad are together and in a good mood.

So, I waited a few days and one evening when the boys were out, Mum, Dad and I had tea together. When we were chatting after pudding (apple crumble and custard) I showed them my phone.

"Gracie gave me this and her dad says I can keep it, but you have to give me permission to use it and I love it, and please may I keep it and I am the only one in my class who hasn't got a phone (not entirely true but nearly) and it's not fair." I said this all at once in a garble.

"What?" said Mum — clearly not impressed

"Let me see," said Dad — he was clearly impressed by the phone. I think it is better than the one he has.

"We agreed, James, that mobile phones were for when they were in senior school, and to let April have one now would not be fair to the boys," said Mum.

I kept quiet as they discussed the issue — to-and-fro. Sometimes I thought Dad was winning but most times it was Mum.

They reached a compromise. As part of my eleventh birthday present, they would get a contract and a sim card, and I could use the phone. This was not too long before I go to senior school. But I had to be sensible. There were to be no endless chats with Gracie and games would be strictly supervised by Dad. I put in that if there was ever a time Mum could not pick me up from school, she could ring me up and I could wait and be safe in the school library instead of standing by myself at the gates. I also said that things were different for girls and they needed to be kept very safe — safer than boys. And I would be safer with a mobile phone.

"Where did you hear that?" said Mum.

"Everybody knows it and we are always told not to talk to strangers or get in strange cars — especially at the school gates."

That clinched it. I had a mobile phone and it would be useable on my birthday.

Another successful rebellion aim. Something is bound to go wrong soon though; this is just too good.

Football

Football is a big thing in our house. To Mum's despair we have a Sky TV sports contract, and every week, when there is a big football match on TV, various combinations of the 4 males in my house sit down together and watch. The way Dad and the boys talk, you would think the guys on TV paid to talk about football know nothing — especially referees, who all seem to need new glasses, it seems. And what is VAR? Adam is part of these male gatherings once again — since Aimee had ditched him. He still looks very sad though.

Sometimes I sit with them. I am reluctantly impressed sometimes when they say "That's a mistake," and then the chap on the TV says "A mistake by so and so…" And goals are fun — they all jump up and celebrate if their team scores. I would like to know more about football and I asked Mum if she could find me a team to join.

"Why on earth do you want to be part of that mindless physical brutish world?" she said. No pursed lips but the idea clearly horrified her.

"It can't be that bad — Dad likes it, and so does Grandad." I replied.

Another tack — "Haven't you enough to do — library visits, Scottish Country Dancing, piano?"

Another cleverer tack, "What does Gracie think of this new fad?"

"I haven't asked her."

"Well, see what Gracie thinks and then come back to me," and she disappeared out of the room quickly before I could give her another good reason why I should play football.

To be honest, I wasn't all that keen on playing football, it was too physical and dirty and people got hurt, but I did want to understand it more so that I could come out with clever comments when I was watching it with Dad and the boys. But I didn't say that, and how else can you understand if you don't do it yourself?

I had a chat with Gracie and she thought I was bonkers to want to risk life-and-limb (where did she hear that phrase?) playing a pointless game that involved moving a ball with your feet on grass.

"But how do I understand it more?" I said.

"I dunno — just concentrate more when you are watching it with your dad and ask questions and don't they do replays or something?" she said very sensibly and looked at me as if I was completely daft.

So that was that. I didn't go to football training but I found a book in the library called 'Football for Dummies' that would help me understand it better. There was also a book there called 'Football is for Girls; A Modern Chick's Guide to understanding the game' — I thought that one could wait. I didn't say anything to Mum about my chat with Gracie and I think she thought that she had won the argument — which I suppose she had.

I was sad that I didn't have a go at football but the

expense would have been huge when I look at all the kit the boys seem to need. This was part of my rebellion that did not succeed but that felt okay — and Mum was relieved. But football is for girls too and perhaps later on I might have a go — I hope so.

I did watch football on TV more closely as a result of all this — I can now identify when there will be a corner and not a goal kick, I know when to say, "That was a free header." I can understand the little triangles that are formed when they are passing the ball, and I can say with authority to Grandad (the rest would scoff), that Barcelona are excellent at making little triangles with the ball. And I have a favourite footballer and a favourite team — my team is Newcastle United because it is ages since they have won anything, and my favourite footballer is Kevin de Bruyne because he has a nice name but he plays for a different team — I think.

I didn't scream and shout at this 'defeat', and it made me think that perhaps I am more like what my mum would like me to be than I realise. Or perhaps I am growing up and changing, and all things are possible. Quite honestly the thought of running about for ages and getting filthy and bruised, and possibly ending up with broken bones did not appeal, but I am enjoying it more now I understand more.

Perhaps golf would suit?

Appendicitis

I have been in hospital! I have had appendicitis! I had to have an emergency operation to take out my appendix which Dad's computer says is finger-shaped and not needed generally. Also, and this is very exciting — appendicitis can be caused by a trapped bit of poo.

I'll start from the beginning. I had been having tummy pains for a few days, not too bad but becoming more regular. I didn't think too much about it as I hadn't been to the loo (for a poo) for a couple of days, and Mum thought that once I had pooed it all out, it would be ok. But the stuff she gave me to help me poo didn't work and the pain got worse and stayed, instead of going away. Painkillers didn't work and then I was sick all over the kitchen floor. I thought my tummy was going to burst and I was crying and screaming. Even the boys were worried.

So, Mum and Dad drove me immediately to our hospital. Adam was left in charge of the twins and I remember Dad saying that if there was a "hint or suspicion" of any trouble when he got back, all three would be grounded with no allowance for a month.

Even in awful pain, I was thinking that if they were grounded, they would not need any allowances. (So, they do get allowances rather than pocket money. I thought as much.)

Anyway, once in hospital they quickly diagnosed that I had appendicitis and they operated straight away before the thing burst. That meant I now have four little holes under a huge plaster rather than one big hole that would have had to be made had the appendix burst. Apparently, what I had is called keyhole surgery. So, do they use a key to fix things or is the hole they make shaped like a keyhole? I must ask someone.

Mum stayed with me and Dad went home to get me some bathroom stuff and nighties for me, and stuff for Mum who said she was not leaving the hospital until she was sure I would be okay. (Yes, she actually said that!) So, Dad rushed off to get stuff — toiletries and things — and check on the boys who unfortunately were not grounded or had their allowances stopped.

I can't remember much after that until I woke up in a single room with Mum staring at me looking so worried. (Yes — I know, it's unbelievable). My tummy was still sore but it was a different sort of sore — a better sort of sore if that is possible.

I stayed in hospital a couple of days — Mum would not let me have any visitors, not even Gracie who I knew would be worried, and certainly not the brothers who apparently were quite worried. Hmmm, I'm not sure I believe that. But Dad came in before and after work, and Mum never budged.

I am home now and lying in bed. And am very sleepy all the time. The tummy pain is less but still there, and I have to be very careful and not be too active and not stretch the wound — four holes under a big plaster. I will have to have a couple of weeks off school.

Gracie has been allowed to see me. The first thing she said was "Oh April — please don't die," and she burst into tears. Poor Gracie, she must have these thoughts about her mum all the time.

Dad was with me at the time and he very sensibly told Gracie all that had happened as if she was a grown up, explaining what appendixes were and that we really do not need them as man has evolved so much (what does evolved mean?) so when they have to come out it is generally okay. The danger is that if not caught early enough, they might burst and that would mean a bigger operation. Luckily my appendix hadn't burst and it was all very straight forward, and I would soon be as good as new.

Dad is so good at this sort of thing. He reassured Gracie and told her the facts so she could understand everything — and she stopped crying.

And Gracie brought me amazing 'Get well soon' presents from her and her mum and dad. They sent me two DVD's — the old and new 'Mary Poppins' films, and the book by PL Travers. But the present came with a task — I had to write a report comparing and contrasting the two films and the book, and then I had to decide which was the best and give my reasons for this decision. Well, that should keep me busy while I am off school.

The new nurse/nanny/housekeeper has started and Gracie said she would tell me all about her at her next visit, as my mum had said she could not stay too long as I tired easily.

And Mum was right — after Gracie's visit, I fell asleep.

Adam, Alfie and Albie have been lovely through all this but I dare say they are still under the threat of being grounded and no allowance for a month. They contributed to a lovely present — it was from all of them including Grandad. They gave me a small TV with a DVD attached for my room. I might look at the older 'Mary Poppins' film tomorrow, the one with Julie Andrews who must be very old by now.

As for Grandad, he comes and visits and just holds my hand while I doze, and we play dominoes until the next doze comes along. He doesn't say much, just occasionally holds my hand tighter.

The Scottish grandparents sent me shortbread which Mum scoffed at, but which is actually very nice, especially with a glass of warm milk. I have to be careful what I eat and I have to eat stuff that helps me poo easily. Of course, I am enjoying any number of Marks and Spencer's Luxury Hot Cross Buns while I recover. The rebellion seems inappropriate at the moment as they are all being so lovely.

Pyjamas!

I have already told you that I wear nightdresses —
usually of the little-girly sort, chosen by Mum. While I
am in bed with my wound and developing scar, I am
wearing a hateful nighty, and a pair of knickers. The
knickers were bought by Mum and yes, they are pink and
frilly and gruesome. The knicker elastic really irritates
the wound area and surrounding skin. In fact, the waist
band goes straight across the middle of my dressing and
makes what is sore even more sore. It's bonkers that I
have to explain the problem to mum and dad– and they
are supposed to be sensible adults looking after me. It
really is horrible and uncomfortable.

So, first of all I explained the problem; that my
knickers were not helping me get better — they were too
tight over my wound — but I still needed something to
keep my plaster in place. I then asked, an inspired ask, if
I say so myself, if I could borrow some of the boys'
pyjamas, as they would be loose in all the right places but
would keep my plaster secure? This was immediately
rejected, as the boys' pyjamas look as if they have been
playing football in them no matter how often Mum finds
them to wash — usually in a hot white wash.

So, I took a deep breath and said, "Please may I have
my own pyjamas so that the elastic will be higher up on

my waist and there is still a cover for my plaster?" This was directed at both Mum and Dad when they were both in the room and honestly, the pyjama request was not part of my rebellion. I just wanted to be more comfortable — and feel safe. I hated it when the nightdress rode up around my waist and bothered the plaster — or— dressing, as I think it is called.

Mum was reluctant as expected, but Dad thought it a good idea and offered to go and get some before the shops closed. I managed to say to him before he left and when Mum had nipped downstairs to get me some milk — "Please remember Dad that I am nearly a teenager and please don't buy pyjamas for little girls."

He winked at me.

I am now the proud owner of three pairs of pyjamas — one to wear, one just in case there are problems, and one in the wash. Their material is blue and white squares with a blue, white and red collar and four red buttons down the jacket, pale purple and white stripes with very jazzy white buttons, and finally one with little rainbows scattered all over. This last one is okay, just okay, but I reckon it was mainly to please Mum.

I am still wearing a girly dressing gown but this is getting a little small so I reckon that will have to be replaced soon. My slippers are awful — their design is the *Frozen* film, Anna on one slipper and Elsa on the other — I have never really liked them. And they still fit — drat! But never mind, my gorgeous pyjamas make up for everything else.

As I recover, my days are spent in bed or downstairs on the sofa. I read a lot but after a few pages I just drop off. At the moment I am reading *Roman Mysteries* by

Caroline Lawrence. We are learning about the eruption of the volcano Vesuvius years and years ago and what happened to Pompeii and Herculaneum. It is really interesting stuff. I am also doing my 'Mary Poppins' task, and I pay a lot of dominoes. A twin, I forget which one, lent me an old iPod with music that I listen to through earphones. It was a lovely idea but some of the music is so loud and weird and disturbing, that I tend not to listen to it too much. It gave me nightmares but I didn't tell anyone.

Mum took some time off work initially, she works part-time in an office doing stuff, but after a week I was left in the care of Grandad during the day. I was much better by then, and after 2 weeks I was ready to go back to school.

Gracie visited as often as she could. The new nanny/nurse/housekeepers have started. The Pritchards have employed two carers to share the work and they seem okay — so far. They are still finding their way around the house and getting to know Gracie's mum's needs. Gracie misses Julia though and she clearly feels more worried for her mum nowadays who might be getting more ill. This is an awful thought.

I feel I have to get better quickly just as much for Gracie as for anyone else. And I am getting bored now. I am ready to return to school and tell everyone that I was ill because a piece of poo got trapped in my tummy. There might have been a different and proper explanation for my tummy pain, but I like mine best.

And who would have thought that appendicitis could result in one of my rebellion aims — pyjamas of my very own — and pyjamas without flowers or fairies.

Thoughts about Mum

While I was ill, Mum was amazing. She was loving and there were no demands made that I struggled with and felt that "it's not fair". The old feelings of guilt have returned now I am well and back at school, and at the moment I haven't too much to grumble about.

My mum must be okay really. Some of the others at school really hate their mums — and their dads — and they hate everything they suggest or ask or do, and when they hate things so much, they have a tantrum and shout and scream until they get their own way. I would never get away with anything like that. If I even tried it, one or all of my brothers would sit on me — and Dad would be so disappointed. So, anything like that is out of the question for me — nothing is that important — yet.

Gracie calls these girls "Complete arses." Once she followed up one of their outbursts with "You have no idea how lucky you are," and rushed out of the room. I followed her and found her crying under the gym stairs.

Gracie's mum is very ill and may not live for as long as Gracie needs her to live. She is okay at the moment but the worry is always there — it never goes away. Gracie said she is always scared when she goes home in case her mum is back in hospital and might not come out for ages — or at all.

Hearing these "complete arses" being so mean about their mums gets Gracie so cross and upset.

And this makes me feel bad — again — about the ongoing 'April Rebellion'. I know it is what I need to do but... And I feel bad about Gracie and that I have so much of everything that she would love to have herself.

But I will carry on carefully, and oddly enough, so far, my successes have not caused too much trouble and I think that Mum and I are getting on much better as a result of all these changes. I hope she sees this too.

Builders and decorators

Hooray! It is official. Grandad is moving in with us. Mum and Dad have decided that we should have the big loft converted into two bedrooms for the twins with a shared shower and loo. I said that a shower was a waste of time and money because, as far as I could see, they never had a wash. Grandad will then have their room. I offered to move into the new roomy loft but Mum and Dad said "No,"— it was time the twins had a room each and they might fight less if separated.

Grandad is going to help with the costs and he has said that there had to be rules.

He will be a bigger part of the family but not altogether, because he has got too used to his own peace and quiet. So, he would like his room (which he is also contributing towards) to be a sitting room and bedroom, and with a sink so he could make a cup of tea without coming downstairs. This new home will be his bedsit.

He will be happy with a single bed and all his double beds from home can go to the tip — although Adam said he would like Grandad's double bed in his room and there was plenty of room for it. (I suspect this will be followed by another private chat in the dining room.)

He would like two armchairs for visitors (I asked for three armchairs so Gracie can visit also) and a decent-sized coffee table for when he and I play dominoes.

He would also like his own sink for washing and shaving. He likes what he calls a wet shave with a bristly brush and scary old-fashioned razor and takes care — and ages — with his morning routine. He also knows what the chaos in our one bathroom is like in the mornings. Thankfully the loo is separate so there are not too many problems, and there is a spare loo downstairs for emergencies. Mum thought that a very good idea as she didn't want the twins experimenting with Grandad's razor blades when they start shaving — and, knowing them, having accidents that involve a lot of blood and mess.

He would like people to knock before they came into his room — he might be asleep and just want to be peaceful.

We all agreed and the builders will arrive soon.

The first job is to empty the loft of years of junk and treasures. Mum's and Dad's schoolbooks were there with curly edges. All our baby things were there — toys and clothes — especially my stuff. Mum said the boys' stuff was not worth keeping as the twins had a lot of Adam's old stuff — which they then wrecked. But there was a suitcase filled with my baby clothes and toys — all lovingly wrapped in tissue paper and packed so very carefully. And they were all in such good condition.

Mum said "I can't get rid of these." There were a few tears as she said this and she was touching the tiny outfits so lovingly. Dad gave her a cuddle and said "One day, perhaps there might be another little girl in the family who might like these." Mum nodded and put them back very carefully.

In the short term they decided that the things in the loft that had to stay, that they absolutely could not throw out (probably everything), could go to Grandad's house until he decided what to do with it.

If the bedsit is a bad idea and Grandad misses his own home too much we are keeping his house in case he decides to go back — even for a just a little while from time to time. And then when all the aunts and uncles and cousins come to stay, there is plenty of room for them all to stay.

This is an expensive way of doing things but Grandad said they could do it for a little while until things were settled.

There is room for a bit of rebellion in all of this. There will be a huge mess upstairs for ages, especially as there needs to be a proper staircase up to the loft — now called the twins' annexe or the 'AA Suite' (pathetic). I waited until mum and dad were in a good mood and suggested that it might be an idea to decorate my room at the same time so that we didn't have to create more horrible mess at a later date. "And we might get a good deal from the decorator as he is doing so much," I said in hope.

Mum looked at me suspiciously and I looked at her innocently. No way could there be a sneaky plan underneath all this planning.

Dad agreed and then I said— "Perhaps Mum, we could look at wallpaper together to get something we both like." A brilliant idea, I thought

"Perhaps," she said — reluctantly.

I took this as a 'yes' and ran for the Laura Ashley catalogue. It can be no surprise that Mum is a great fan of Laura Ashley and all those flowery prints.

You'll never guess what I picked. I rather liked a wallpaper called 'Wild Meadow' — lots of wild flowers scattered about the wall. It was bright and cheery, and my existing curtains would go with it nicely.

Mum was surprised and she liked it too and said it would look very nice.

Now how can that be rebellion? I have what I wanted and there was no battle — just agreement. And Dad was so pleased with my/our choice too.

Of course, the twinsF then said that they wanted to pick wallpaper for the 'AA Suite'. It was not fair as I was only ten — "Nearly eleven," I muttered. Both Mum and Dad said absolutely no — they would have paint that could easily be repaired and no, they could not have black or navy blue paint on the walls. Those two idiots really have a lot to learn about rebellion. They should talk to their sister.

A death

While all the building work was going on, Dad learned from New Zealand that his mum had died. The psychotherapist rang up to tell him. She had not wanted any fuss and there would not be a funeral, so it was not worthwhile Dad, his brother and sisters, and Grandad going out to New Zealand. And that was that — the psychotherapist rang off.

Dad rang back straight away for more details. He was both upset and cross with the psychotherapist for not getting in touch earlier, and he was quite harsh as he demanded to know what had happened. I have never seen Dad like that.

Grandma had been having headaches for a while and she then had a stroke — I didn't know what that meant as we stroke Potts all the time and he is fit and well. Dad explained it was a big brain bleed and there is no cure when it is so serious. Anyway, it all happened very quickly and there was no way any of her English relatives could get out to see her.

Dad had then to tell Grandad. Mum asked if he wanted her to go with him but he said no — it was something he had to do himself and then he would ring my aunties and uncle.

It was a few hours before he came back and it was

clear he had been crying. He just said Grandad was okay and wanted to be alone for a while but he would come for tea tomorrow. I thought "Would a Marks and Spencer's Luxury Hot Cross Bun help?" but didn't say anything.

It all feels odd. I should be sad but I am not. She was my grandma but I hardly ever saw her. There were a few pictures, but once she and the psychotherapist left for New Zealand we were in touch hardly at all. The three brothers felt the same. Adam had known her for longer and he just shrugged, muttered something I didn't hear, and went upstairs to his room. The twins looked baffled. Why were we so upset about someone who was not part of our lives?

Dad said nothing and just left the room at this point and went into the garden. They looked even more baffled at this.

Mum said to them, "Grandma was once very important to your dad, and even if they were not in touch much, he still has happy memories of her and she is still his mum — let him be sad and try and understand why he is sad."

At that they nodded, but still looked baffled.

Dad was sitting quietly on the garden seat so I took him a Marks and Spencer's Luxury Hot Cross Bun filled with butter and cheddar cheese, and my mum added a glass of single malt whiskey.

"Thank you, April," he said in a very quiet voice. So, I sat with him for a while and held his hand.

After a while he said "I think Grandad will need you to play dominoes tomorrow".

I nodded.

Grown-ups are very strange. You think they are always in control of everything then something comes along and they are the ones that need looking after. Perhaps being a grown-up isn't as easy as I thought, and perhaps that is why they have to be so controlling and careful with their children — because nothing can be relied on, ever, and life is so worrying.

Next day I went to see Grandad before he came for tea. The dominoes were ready on the table.

I said, "I am sorry about Grandma".

He nodded and said, "Yes — it has been a long time since we were together but I am sad too. I remember the good times and I am sad that the good times couldn't continue. I am sad for what wasn't to be — and that is okay. I am happy that she found what she wanted even if it was a long way away, but I am sad she wasn't happy enough with me — us. But I am so lucky, Littley, I have all of you and dominoes. I will be okay and so will your Dad. Double-six to start."

At tea, Dad opened a bottle of wine and we drank a toast to absent friends — and family. I had orange juice.

Another list of things that are getting in the way of my rebellion

1. Adam has a new girlfriend. He is not officially finished with Aimee but he has been seen with someone else and I know who she is. She is the older sister of a girl in my class, she is called Elsa (the girlfriend is called Elsa, the girl in my class is called Eliza — perhaps that family had an 'E' problem like we had an 'ABC' problem) and she is in the year below Adam.

Aimee found out and she has unfriended him on social media and made all her friends unfriend him, I think that is the word for it — I will check with Gracie. Adam is furious and his friends total on social media has gone down by loads.

Aimee then came to our house and dumped all his stuff that he had left at her house, no pyjamas of course. She left them on the step and she had been at the whole lot with scissors.

"Hell hath no fury like a woman scorned" quoted Dad. I asked where that came from — somebody called Congreve apparently — never heard of him.

I had to tell Grandad at the next domino session. Grandad just shook his head and said "Has he now?" Of course, he knows a lot about being dumped and how it feels. As ever the twins are being total rotters and they too have unfriended him and said all sorts of scabby things about him.

Mum and Dad said this had to stop or their mobiles would be confiscated.

The twins are total stinkers — they seem to hate each other but they are very much together when it means being unpleasant to other people, even family. I don't think they deserve a room of their own. Or at least perhaps it is Mum and Dad's plan to get them up there and then take the new ladder to the tip. That would be my solution.

Anyway, they won't be having a ladder up to the 'AA Suite' — it will be a proper staircase. Something to do with fire regulations.

2. Julia, the ex-nanny/nurse/housekeeper is now on her way to Italy. Gracie gets postcards regularly — Paris first, then Monte Carlo, and Nice and Cannes. I looked in the atlas, these are places in the south of France. Julia then went to Spain where she found Madrid, the capital, and Barcelona too busy and too full of tourists, but she then went south and loved Cadiz which was near where Christopher Columbus set off from to find America. She stayed there a week. She is now in Rome and Gracie's dad is working there at the moment, so perhaps they will meet up.

The new nanny/nurse/housekeepers are okay. But Gracie misses Julia heaps, as does her mum.

3. Mum has let me give up piano lessons. It was her idea. I failed Grade II twice and she accepted that her ambition for me to be a concert pianist would not ever happen. And they cost money which was being wasted. I

was a bit sorry that there wasn't a battle between us so that piano lessons ended. But hey ho, perhaps not everything needs a fight and lots of sneaky thoughts. Perhaps you just have to wait and hope.

4. The builders are getting on well. They are busy up in the loft and the decorator has started early on my room. My wallpaper looks amazing and instead of having my old curtains, Mum is making me a pair with matching material. It will look gorgeous and posh. While the decorators are in my room I am staying at Grandad's house. There was a lot of discussion about this and they decided that I was the safest at Grandad's as the boys just could not be trusted not to get up to mischief and worry Grandad.

Mum takes me there at bedtime and comes back for me at breakfast time to have breakfast at home. At weekends I have breakfast with Grandad and then set off for home and the library, and Scottish Country Dancing.

5. I am worried that I do not know enough about pop music. Some of the girls at school are always talking about boy-bands generally and girl-bands generally, and how so and so is so handsome. Am I falling behind? Is my growing up not going along at the right pace? The other girls also know such a lot about 'EastEnders' and 'Hollyoaks' and 'Coronation Street'. None of these are allowed in our house and the TV goes off after 'Pointless' and the 'Six-o' clock News' so we can all have supper together. The twins usually have excuses and wriggle out of these meals, so it is often just me and Mum and Dad, and, at the moment, a still sad Adam. Even Marks and Spencer's Luxury Hot Cross Buns aren't helping. And to

makes things worse, Esme has today ended their brief friendship. He is such hard work to be with at the moment. Also, he has suddenly come out in a heap of spots with yellow tops. Mum, of course, has bought him all sorts of lotions and creams and facewashes but they don't seem to be helping much. Every time she sees him, she says, "Don't you dare squeeze your spots," and he looks at her then with such dislike.

Might he be planning a rebellion, I wonder?

I must remember to talk to Gracie about pop music and soap operas and spots.

Grandad moves in

The builders and decorators have finished. My room looks gorgeous with new wallpaper and matching curtains, and we have moved my furniture around a bit so it looks like a completely new room. I have a blow-up bed under my bed in case Gracie comes to stay and the two best bits are that there is definitely less pink and there are more books on a shelf that Adam made. He is almost pleasant these days.

The twins have already destroyed the new loft rooms. They fought over who had which room and we hear them fight over who has the bathroom first in the mornings. I have been up to have a look and it is disgusting — for a start they are totally unable to flush the loo — there are always unflushed poos and pees up there. Yuck. The thought that they may fight less if separated was clearly not sensible.

Their room has been made into Grandad's bedsit and newly decorated, it looks amazing. He has everything he needs — a single bed, two armchairs (with a fold up chair if Gracie visits), a sink, and a table with a kettle and toaster, and cups and saucers and plates. There is even a tiny fridge for his milk and a few cans of lager.

When Grandad first moved in, he came with just a small suitcase. He was still worried he had not made the right decision but we made a fuss. He had to cut a ribbon across his door and we all had champagne (although I think it was prosecco which is not so expensive), even me. So, he had a huge welcome. For a while he went back to his own house for a night or two, and then for a few hours, but this became less and less and now Grandad is with us all the time — but we don't point it out. Dad says Grandad will tell us himself when he has made his mind up what to do. It is a big decision for him and all we can do is make him welcome — as if we would do anything else, even the boys scoffed at that thought.

And this all helps with my rebellion because I know I have an ally in the same house who loves me. Did I mention I bought him some new dominoes for his new room — with coloured spots? He was thrilled with his new present and the old dominoes are at his old place.

My eleventh birthday

I must admit I was dreading this. I thought I would be given lots of pink surprises, and the boys, on purpose, find me the most gruesome, pink plastic nonsense that they know I have to say "Thank you — that is lovely," for but hate deep down. These presents will soon be hidden in my bedroom and forgotten. I won't say they were thoughtless presents, clearly a lot of thought went into them but they were not very kind thoughts.

As hoped for, Dad gave me my mobile with a contract and a sim card. It was useable straight away so I rang up Gracie and said a huge thank you. Grandad and Mum gave me money — actual cash — to go shopping with. Wow – and there was enough cash to buy some really nice things

The Saturday after my birthday and after the library and Scottish Country Dancing, I went into town with Mum. I overheard a conversation between her and Dad before we set off.

Dad said — "Let her choose, Cate. Please let her do it herself."

Mum said, "But what if what she buys is awful and never gets worn and is a waste of money?"

Dad said, "Then she will learn from her mistakes and she will have wasted a good birthday present"

Mum said, "But…"

Quickly followed by,

"Please, Cate," from Dad. "She is growing up and has to learn to make some decisions herself and learn what not to do if she gets it wrong, and this is a safe enough decision."

A reluctant "OK," followed from Mum.

So off we went.

I bought two books. *Little Women* by Louisa May Allcott which had on the cover four sisters wearing pretty dresses, two of them pink. Mum said it was a classic and was pleased with my choice. I was surprised by that choice too, as stories about girls in pretty dresses are not my favourites but it is also about the American Civil War, so it can't be all bad. The other book was by David Walliams. Mum isn't keen on him when he is on TV but she agreed he is a good writer.

So far, so good.

Then I bought some clothes – some really stylish patent-leather ankle boots, some amazing leg-hugging jeans and a long shirt in a material with all sorts of colours and patterns in it. Mum loved the boots, was okay with the jeans and was horrified with the shirt but said nothing.

I am not having a party but Mum and Dad are taking me and Gracie to Pizza Express for a meal and I will wear all my new clothes.

When I got home, I tried them on for Dad and Grandad. They were watching football together. I felt and looked so good and grown up.

Grandad said "You look a real treat, Littley — but I

wish you weren't growing up so quickly," he has said that before to me. Mum said nothing but nodded, but she looked pleased with my choices and how I looked — I think. Dad looked pleased but also a bit worried. I will ask him why one day.

Gracie arrived. She had good news. Julia is coming back at the end of the month. Her mum and dad are very pleased and they have told the new nanny/nurse/housekeeper that they will need another job soon. But they did it very nicely of course.

Gracie's present to me was all sorts of things for the bathroom in a nice bag — body wash, shampoo, conditioner, body cream, hand cream, and lots of other interesting bottles and pots. She really is a gorgeous friend.

We had a lovely meal at Pizza Express. Gracie and I had a starter, a main course and then we squeezed in a pudding that we shared (chocolate cake). Mum and Dad had a starter and a main course and they had some wine, and they all made a toast to "April who is now eleven years old."

And I have to say I love all my new clothes, even the bright shirt that Dad says he needs sunglasses to look at. Gracie was very impressed and nodded approvingly when I did a twirl before we set off.

So far so good with the rebellion, I think. I have had a number of successes which are great but I do wish Mum wasn't so gloomy after each success. I can understand why she is as she is but I would like there to be a bit more understanding about why I am as I am. One more year and I will be in senior school and I bet that will bring along a lot more things to fight about.

As I see it, as soon as you get to senior school you grow in height and get boobs and you have to wear bras. At the moment I have nothing that would fit into a bra and I am happy enough with that as I sleep on my tummy. When I was getting better from appendicitis I had to sleep on my back and it was awful. The senior school girls seem to know everything about everything. I hope I can catch up a bit and be a bit more prepared in my last year at junior school. Oh heck.

The summer holidays

Julia is back and Gracie and her family are so happy. And so is Julia — she said she missed them all. She brought presents — a lovely Italian leather bag for Gracie, a Murano glass bowl for Gracie's mum (Murano is in Venice and it is famous for making glass things), a book about Pompeii for Gracie's dad, and a gorgeous Italian leather purse for me. How very, very, kind.

Julia is looking after Gracie's mum while Gracie and her dad go on an adventure holiday in Cornwall — horse riding, and fell walking, and surfing, and walking, and camping, and all sorts. I was asked along too but Mum thankfully said "No" before I could disappoint Gracie. It was all too active for me and I would hate it if I couldn't keep up.

Mum is learning at last and having good ideas about what I should or should not do.

Mum also said no because we were off to the Scottish grandparents' B and B for just a week, then we were going to a big caravan site for another week with all sorts of activities — and hopefully fun.

Adam did not want to come. He is now seventeen and has a job in the local pub/restaurant washing dishes and clearing tables. Grandad says he, Adam, will be fine and that he, Grandad, would ring and tell them straight away if there was trouble. Mum was not happy with this idea — and neither was Dad. We have to be back for his GCSE results in August. That will be fun — not! His love life is pretty quiet at the moment as he is working all the time. He is saving his earnings to buy a car — his seventeenth birthday present was driving lessons. Dad takes him out sometimes and comes back and has a single malt whisky before anything else.

Also, Grandad said he and Adam would look after Potts who usually goes into prison (boarding kennels) for this annual holiday.

So, there were just five of us who headed north — to the midges and haggis and the Loch Ness monster, and where I could show off my Scottish Country Dancing.

The holiday was okay — the first week was tricky as Mum is never happy in the B and B. She says it is not like being at home but it is like a hotel, and you can't relax and you have to be very careful with all these carefully-placed knickknacks. The twins had a few accidents of course and I think the Scottish grandparents were glad to see the back of us. I also think Mum and Dad were glad to move on. That is so sad for Mum but when I asked her why it wasn't a lot of fun being there, she just said, "It is what it is, April, and there's nothing we can do to change it."

The second week in the caravan was great fun. There were bike rides and swimming in a very cold lake (loch?), and crazy golf, and even pitch and putt golf that we all had a go on. I also made friends with a couple of other girls — but I missed Gracie. The midges weren't too bad and the weather was okay.

In no time, we were heading south to home and GCSE results. Grandad was very pleased to see us back — as was Potts. I didn't see Adam for three days because of the shifts he works at the pub, but according to Grandad their time together had been OK. I'm not sure Mum and Dad believed him.

Adam's results came in. He did okay. He took ten and passed eight. Of these eight, five were scrape passes, he just made it and then three were okay passes in things he was interested in — sciences and maths. He failed English, which were two exams, and something called technical drawing. It could have been a lot worse.

Next year he wants to leave school and go to the local college. I would imagine there will be a lot of private chats in the dining room with Dad about that in the next few weeks. But oddly enough, Adam, these days, is almost nice to me. I'm not sure what to make of that and find it all very suspicious.

The twins are still awful, in every sense, and they still fight even though they each have their own private space in the loft. As expected, the new loft is already a complete mess, and Mum seems to be getting on at them these days more than me.

An awful time

Gracie is very unhappy — she is totally and absolutely miserable and sad, and in tears all the time. It was noticed at school where she was appalling to teachers and some of the other girls in our class. She was screaming and shouting and kicking things, and using the most amazing horrible language that really surprised the teachers, and before they could do anything about it, she ran off — without her coat. Her mum was told and her dad was home at the time so he set off to look for her — in the park, her favourite shops.

I found her in our garden shed. She rang me and told me she was there but I hadn't to tell anyone. "Just come home and act normal," she said.

When I got home, Mum was there so I said I was just going into the garden for a bit.

"Really?" she said, clearly this was something new but she didn't think anything more of it and she just told me to put on a coat.

I found Gracie in the shed, hidden behind a pile of deckchairs, crouched down with her arms wrapped around her legs and her tear stained face looking out over the top of her knees.

"What has happened?" I asked. "Is it your mum?" I must admit I feared the worst — that her mum had died.

"No, not that. Mum is okay. It's Dad and Julia. I found them kissing," and more tears flooded down her face.

"No, that's impossible." I didn't know what else to say and I too crouched down and started to cry.

"It's true. I went down to the kitchen last night quite late for a glass of milk and there they were in the kitchen, having the biggest snog ever. I hate them both."

"Does your mum know?"

"I don't know. I want to tell her but she will be so upset. I'm not going home. Can I stay here for a while?"

"We will have to ask my mum and dad first — you can't really hide in the shed all the time."

She nodded and I went to get Mum.

Mum was very good. She listened to Gracie's story with no interruption and then asked if she could ring Gracie's mum and dad and tell them she was safe as they would be every scared and worried. Then Gracie would have to go home, but my mum would take her, and try and sort things out.

Gracie nodded and off they went with Gracie still crying, but not as noisily or wetly. Mum came home after a little while and just said to me "She'll be fine, don't worry."

But I did worry, and didn't sleep, and was constantly checking my mobile for messages, but there was nothing.

I didn't hear from Gracie for two days. She wasn't at school and although I was tempted to send messages Mum said I shouldn't and that I should wait for Gracie to contact me. She was right.

The following Saturday after the library and Scottish

Country Dancing, we came home and Gracie and her dad were parked outside our house. Gracie and I got out of our cars at the same time and hugged and hugged. Gracie's dad said, "I will be back for you in a couple of hours if that is okay?" looking at my mum.

"Of course," she said and he drove off.

Thankfully all the boys were out so Gracie and I went straight up to my room. She told me what had happened. She, her Dad, her mum and Julia had had a long talk. Gracie's dad had said time and time again that he was sorry and so had Julia. He admitted that he had feelings for Julia but they were no way as strong as his feelings for Gracie's mum and Gracie. They both said they had got carried away with Julia being so pleased to be back. Julia then said she had missed us all but would leave permanently if that would help the family

Then Gracie's mum said something much unexpected. She said she didn't want Julia to leave them. Their need for Julia and her many skills were made clear during her time in Europe — no matter how well or hard her replacement had worked, it was just not the same and not as good. And she would need Julia's skills more and more in the future as she was getting more ill. And this was the big surprise, she said she didn't mind Gracie's dad and Julia having a friendship but please keep it under control — while she was alive.

Gracie said that the thought that her mum might die was far worse than any snog, and that keeping Mum happy and as well as possible was, had to be, her, her dad's, and Julia's priority. It was very difficult and she still was not at ease with her dad and Julia. Her dad had spoken to her alone since and told her that yes, he was fond of Julia, they shouldn't have kissed, it was a mistake, and that he loved his wife more than anything in the world, and Gracie had to believe that.

Gracie said she had been so tempted to ask her dad if he and Julia had kissed a lot before the time when she caught them at it and also to ask if they had snogged in Rome, but she didn't. It wouldn't do any good. They just had to think of her mum and in any case, she wasn't sure she wanted to know.

"So, what is next?" I asked.

"We go on as we were as well as we can. But I'll be watching out to make sure they don't break their promise," she replied.

I just nodded. Shortly after that, her dad arrived back and beeped his car horn. She left without Mum or me saying anything to her dad.

"All okay?" asked Mum when I went downstairs.

"Sort of — I think — I hope," I said, and burst into tears. After a few nose and eye wipes. "I hope we never have a nanny/nurse/housekeeper. It would be so awful if you or Dad decided you liked someone else."

She chuckled and said "With you four, Dad and I haven't the time, money or energy for anything like that — although if Jonas Kauffman came my way, I might be tempted."

"Who?" I asked with alarm.

"He's a German opera singer — come and hear a lovely voice", and off we went to hear some amazing music.

And he did have a lovely voice — and he looked good too, but Dad looks better.

Another list

1. I am now in senior school and I feel very grown-up, despite being in the first year, the lowest of the low. I go to school on the bus with the twins — they ignore me — and so far, have always remembered to ring Mum from the school yard on my precious mobile to tell her I am safely there. It used to be that Gracie looked after me and I looked up to her. It's the other way around now. She is like my shadow and is always asking me if such and such is okay. The mess at home is getting her down and she is off school more often than she ever used to be with coughs and colds. I think she is okay — she just wants to be with her mum and keep an eye on her dad. When he is not away, she usually manages to be at home more. It is so sad that she doesn't trust her dad.

2. Mum and I have had a chat (in my room, not in the dining room) about boys, sex and periods. It sounds so awful — I think I will adopt children. I just couldn't go through any of that malarkey and I will probably die when my periods start — they sound doubly awful — and I might have them for forty years — or more. How gross!

3. Adam is at college doing an apprenticeship and he is very happy there. He has a lot of new friends and a lot of friends who are girls but nobody special — yet. He spends a lot of time at college and goes in on his days off

to help with the students who have difficulties. That is very kind and not like Adam at all. He has passed his driving test and all his work savings and birthday and Christmas presents, probably forever, from Mum and Dad and Grandad, have been spent on a little car. The insurance was terrifyingly high because of his age and I reckon the insurance people knew his history and figured he would be a risk. The nice thing is, he is always willing to take me and fetch me from Gracie's and he does the same for her.

4. The twins are a surprise. Apparently at school, they are well-behaved and work very hard, and amazingly, are liked by the other kids and teachers. And they always get high marks in whatever they do. Does the school really know those two rotters?

I asked Mum about this and she said she and Dad knew they were both bright kids, they had known since the twins started school, and they always worked very hard.

"How come I didn't know? How come they are so awful at home?" I then asked.

"Well, you never asked and I think they use home to relax and let off steam," she said. "And they fight because they are always competing with each other — at everything. They hate it when one gets better marks or a better report. It just makes them work much harder".

Well, well, well.

5. Grandad has decided he is happy with us and that he will sell his house one day (Hooray!). So, at weekends he, Mum and Dad, and occasionally me as well, go back to his house to sort out and throw out. And that includes

a lot of stuff from our loft.

A lot of the stuff has gone to the local tip but there is also a lot of stuff that is worth keeping and too good to throw away. My eldest cousin Gareth has spent all his savings on a house. He is engaged to a Jane (who we will meet soon I hope) and Jane is having a baby. How history repeats itself in our family.

So, some of Grandad's big bits of furniture have gone to Gareth's new house. Now they have a home of their own with furniture.

Their baby will be a girl and reluctantly, Mum is sending a lot of my baby stuff to them also. There are a few pieces she refuses to part with but a lot has gone to Gareth and Jane.

Dad is so pleased Grandad will be with us permanently. He always worried that Grandad would decide we were horrible and go back home, where he would not be as safe.

6. Mum has a new job and works full-time. This means that I am on my own more and I have a lot more independence. There is a lot of checking in with her and Dad by mobile, but that is okay and perhaps the need for a rebellion is less at the moment. I reckon this will not last. Also, I end up doing more jobs around the house like preparing tea before Mum gets in so is this a time for an allowance increase?

7. Dad is still Dad. He doesn't change much and I like that.

8. Potts the dog is still Potts the dog. He spends a lot of time with Grandad now Mum is not at home as much. I reckon Potts was the reason Grandad decided to stay

with us. He even has a basket in Grandad's room and a box of treats. Both Potts and Grandad are getting old, they both need less exercise these days and sleep a lot. In fact, sometimes when we get ready to take Potts out for a walk, he looks outside to check the weather and if it doesn't suit, he goes straight back up to Grandad's room. Perhaps he needs to pee less too — Potts that is, not Grandad.

Huge sadness

We had a phone call very early one morning from Gracie's dad and he gave Dad (I think it was Dad) some very sad news. Gracie's mum had died. Julia had gone into Mrs Pritchard's room at about seven a.m. with her morning cup of tea, their usual start to the day, and she found her "unresponsive". I think that was the word. Julia immediately went for Gracie's dad in the next room, who dialled 999 straight after checking Gracie's mum. While he was dialling, Gracie woke up, went into her mum's room and saw the worst thing she would ever see in her life — her mum who would never be able to be her mum again. She immediately burst into loud hysterical tears which brought her dad and Julia rushing into the room. They tried to comfort her but were unsuccessful.

How awful for my gorgeous friend — how horrible, horrible, horrible.

Eventually they rang dad who immediately told mum. Her response was, "We must go at once."

At this point, I was coming downstairs thinking about the day ahead at school and Mum said, "You aren't going to school today — Gracie needs you — and I am not going into work either."

I knew immediately what had happened and silent tears were soon rolling down my face, and I was shaking.

"April," she said. "We are needed. Get ready." This shook me out of my misery and I got my coat.

Mum got a fish pie, a lasagne, and a cake out of the freezer. "They won't have time to cook — or eat today."

And off we went.

That horrible day is just a blur now. I spent most of it holding Gracie tight or holding her hand as she wandered around the house and not saying much. The ambulance men came and a doctor also, who thought he could not be sure, but it was probably a heart attack. There would have to be an autopsy (I thought it was spelled ortopsy) which meant Gracie's mum's body would have to be looked at closely. Forms were filled in.

There was lots of toing and froing. Mum seemed to make endless cups of tea and sandwiches.

Eventually in the evening, Mum and I went home and I cried and cried and cried and Mum didn't/couldn't stop me. Poor, poor Gracie, poor Mr Pritchard, poor Julia and poor me. I went straight to bed. I think Mum gave me something to help me sleep and the next thing I remember, it was tomorrow. I woke in pain, not physical pain, but it felt there was a huge weight on top of me and inside me.

When I went downstairs, I said "Take me to Gracie's." Mum nodded and off we went.

I wasn't at school for the rest of that week. In fact, I stayed at Gracie's house. It would be a while before they could have a funeral, so at the weekend Gracie and her dad went off to a hotel somewhere to have quiet time together — at least they said it was a hotel but it had little cottages in the grounds. Gracie and her dad had one of these and all their food was delivered so Gracie and her dad did not have to mix or be polite to the other guests.

Julia did not go with them saying she wanted to get the house sorted for their return. Mum and I went to see her and found her crying most times.

"It's all my fault," she kept saying.

Mum asked, "Why".

"If I hadn't got fond of them all, including Rob (Mr Pritchard), and she hadn't known, perhaps her heart would have been strong enough to go on beating".

All the comfort in the world and all the medical evidence in the world wouldn't change her mind. But Mum kept an eye on her until Mr Pritchard and Gracie returned home.

The following week I was back at school. All the others wanted to know all about it but I told them to "F-off" and got into trouble — but not too much, the teachers understood.

After a couple of weeks, Gracie came back to school and she seemed less of a person. There was no interest or enthusiasm or anything, and she looked so thin and small.

It was a horrible time and I was so worried about my best pal in all the world. Her grief and sadness just went on and on and on.

Christmas

Christmas was miserable. Gracie was away somewhere hot, Australia, I think. It's not that she didn't tell me, it's just that she and her dad went somewhere cold, Lapland, and didn't like it so they moved on. I might get a postcard telling me where they are but things are different these days. Gracie and I are still friends but she says so little these days — to anyone. Julia is with them wherever they are.

Grandad caught a chill walking Potts the dog and was in bed coughing and spluttering all through Christmas. But he recovered for New Year's Eve and stayed up till five minutes past midnight. I tried to stay up but fell asleep on the sofa at about eleven p.m. and was carried up to bed. I woke up still in my New Year's Eve outfit — a jumpsuit.

Adam was working at the pub again till the early hours and the twins were at a party. I had been invited to a party but I didn't want to go without Gracie. The thought that I might enjoy myself was awful, I wasn't ready for that yet; it felt like betrayal. I was missing my best pal. Even when she was around, I was missing my best pal. Something had changed absolutely and possibly for ever, and I was worried about the future and me and Gracie, and all sorts.

Gracie was still not back when we went back to school, in fact it was early half term before I saw her, although there had been postcards from amazing places — Sydney, the Great Barrier Reef, Auckland, Tahiti, Hawaii, and finally California. They must have heaps of money. Two weeks in damp (usually) Scotland is what we manage.

She finally turned up at my house one Saturday afternoon. She looked different — her hair was shorter and she had clothes that really made you notice that she was much thinner. We talked and finally she told me she wouldn't be returning to school. Dad had found a boarding school where support for young people who had had difficulties was also available. It was academically very good but the support side, I think she used the word "pastoral", was excellent. Gracie thinks this is a good idea as she needs to get away from anything that would remind her of her life with Mum. Her dad and Julia are a couple — and that is okay — but they don't snog in front of her, although she knows they do snog — and other private stuff.

Gracie looked so lost and sad. I cried and cried but she was so cold and hard, and showed no real emotion. Perhaps her emotions have been all used up since her mum died and they have to build up again.

I went to see Gracie at her home but it was not a happy visit. When my dad picked me up from Gracie's, she just said, "Bye then," and closed the door.

All Dad said as we drove away was, "I'm sorry April. This must be horrible for you but I think your friend is struggling. I hope this boarding school is the right place for her."

"Can you talk to her Dad? Can she live with us?" I couldn't believe what I was going through was real. It was horrible — for Gracie.

"I'll try but I can't promise anything. At least I will see her dad and ask how things are."

"Thanks."

But nothing came of this chat.

The rebellion again

I need to get angry about something, to do something new and different, and I have decided that I am not eating meat anymore. I have decided to become vegetarian. The whole idea that we kill animals to feed ourselves is sickening. The food-chain idea from the 'Lion King' just does not work for me anymore. Eating someone else's flesh is horrible.

Mum is not happy about it. She reckons we need to have a variety of nutrition and that includes meat. We actually have shouting disagreements and then I storm off upstairs. Dad tries to use reason but that doesn't work either.

But we came to a reasonable decision where they would not oppose my decision but they wanted proof that I was getting all the necessary nutrition I needed for healthy growth.

Back to the library for books on nutrition and diets, and both Mum and I prepared meals that were good for me — and delicious. We tried all sorts of interesting vegetables and things like Quorn and Tofu, and different things made especially for non-meat-eaters. Some were awful and it was like eating cardboard, but most were worth trying — and I especially liked Linda McCartney's range of ready meals when I or Mum couldn't be bothered to cook. I didn't like the idea that separate meals were having to be cooked so I made the effort to cook my own meals.

What happened was not expected at all. I lost a bit of weight and my skin looked good and my energy was amazing, and somehow, it made the whole Gracie mess easier to deal with.

Then Mum admitted to enjoying these new tastes and joined me in my vegetarianism. That's not supposed to happen when you have a rebellion.

But I am a failed total-vegetarian. After three months or so, I stopped needing to be angry and could be seen nibbling pieces of chicken or ham. The family didn't scoff or talk about it, and slowly I started eating a little more meat from time to time. My diet was mainly vegetarian, as was Mum's, but eventually we felt okay with the occasional meat dish — especially the bacon and fried tomato sandwiches.

Mum thinks my vegetarianism was a reaction to the loss of Gracie and her mum. I had to do something, to change something in my life in some way to make the awfulness more bearable, even though my reasons for becoming vegetarian make a lot of sense without anything awful happening in your life. Slowly I accepted — I will never say got used to — that Gracie might be away for a while, but I always believed she would come back one day. I was missing her and I was missing her mum. I was even missing her dad and Julia, and all this 'missing' stuff takes a while to get used to.

A trip to France

I am good at French. I enjoy the lessons and have even got some books written in easy French from the library. At the moment, I am trying to get through the adventures of 'Babar the Elephant'. So, I was keen to go on a French exchange to Northern France where we stayed with a French family for a week, and later on we did the same for the French boys and girls. There were six of us who went, and the group who went were sort of friends but I was very sad that Gracie wasn't with us; she would have loved this sort of thing.

I was sad to leave the family, even the boys, and even if it was just for a week. We went by coach to Folkestone where we took the tunnel to Calais. That was very exciting, sitting in a bus, miles underneath the English Channel, and after Calais, there was a short drive to Camiers. This drive was long enough and we were all glad that our exchange wasn't in the south of France, even if that part is the glamorous and sunny part of France. All of us were in the area around Camiers — Ste Cécile, Hardelot, and Étaples.

My family were the Blancs, which is white in French, and my exchange partner was Françoise Blanc. She was the same age as me and her English was okay, so from the start we managed to chat. We went to school with our exchange partners and in the evenings the families were to speak to us only in French, even if they spoke English, and they were to take us around the area.

I had a lovely time. It was amazing and for the first time since Gracie's mum had died I felt happier. No, that is not quite right — I felt happier for longer spells. And the Blanc family were gorgeous. Françoise has a younger sister — lucky so-and-so — called Delphine, and Mr and Mrs Blanc (Monsieur et Madame) both worked. Madame Blanc worked in a very stylish dress shop in Le Touquet

We went to Le Touquet, which is very posh with gorgeous shops and cafes. I learned that PG Wodehouse who wrote books about 'Jeeves and Wooster' lived there during the Second World War and was arrested by the Germans when they invaded France. I asked why he didn't go home earlier but no-one knew the answer to that. Le Touquet has a lovely sandy beach but the beach is covered with beach huts and swimming pools and stuff, which I think spoil it. The best beach was at Ste Cécile where there is just a beach and dunes, and a few shops and cafes. The tide goes out for miles and miles, and comes right into the dunes. I took some amazing pictures. We walked from Ste Cécile along the beach to Hardelot but we had to be collected at Hardelot by Mr (Monsieur) Blanc as the tide was right in. In Hardelot, we found what I thought was the best chocolate shop in the world and all my gifts for home were bought in one go.

We also went to Montreuil, a lovely walled-town with battlements, and we walked right round these scary battlements. There was no fence stopping people or dogs falling down a huge drop. That would not happen in

England what with health and safety worries, and in no way would I bring Potts the dog to Montreuil. He would be over like a shot, even if he was on a lead and he would no doubt drag one of us with him — ideally one or both of the twins.

School was tricky as they speak French so very quickly, and time and time again I asked them to speak more slowly, "Lentement, s'il vous plait." Obviously, it was easier doing maths there as we were all very good with French numbers. But they were all very kind and helpful, and that made it okay.

It was a fabulous week. I was sad to leave Françoise and her family, but looked forward to her coming to England. We talked about where she would like to go and she said London. That was a surprise as I have never been to London and I would never have suggested or asked to go to Paris, the French capital city. Mum and Dad will have to think about that one.

But I think I will also remember my trip to France as when I started to be properly happy again. I had a new friend, Françoise, but in no way did she take Gracie's place. Rather, new space had been created in me, and that space for a new friend that did not get in the way of Gracie's space.

The return of Gracie

It is nearly the summer holidays. The need for rebellion has been less in recent months. Adam and the twins muddle on as they usually do, Mum and Dad are much the same, Grandad is getting older and slower, and Potts the dog is as gorgeous as ever.

There has been a change though. In recent weeks I have had a few letters from Gracie — she hasn't used her mobile strangely, almost as if she wants to keep some distance between us. But her letters are longer and seem more cheerful and hopeful.

She has told me that she will finish the year at her boarding school and it has been okay there. Every week she has seen a lady whose work is with children who have a mum or dad who has died, and she has been so helpful. She has talked and cried and been silent, and played games and read books and all sorts with this lady, and she feels a bit better about the fact that her mum is no longer alive. It seems odd but Gracie said that she feels her mum is still with her although she cannot see her or be with her. And she, Gracie, even talks to her mum though she can't reply and that feels OK.

Her dad has asked if she minded if Julia became his permanent girlfriend. Gracie actually replied and said, "Why don't you get married and stop messing about?"

Gosh that was brave. They will get married but not immediately, and Gracie has agreed to be a bridesmaid so long as I could be a bridesmaid too. What do I think? She then said she would be in touch when she got home and perhaps, we could meet up.

Yes, yes, and yes, and more yesses. This letter means that Gracie is once again able to be a friend. I need her friendship and I think she needs mine and is ready, almost, to be a friend again.

I cried when I read the letter and when I showed it to Mum, she cried too. Gracie will be home in a few weeks — hooray times one million. And next year, Gracie will be back at our school — even more hoorays.

It is hard to explain how all this feels. The easiest way I think is to say that everything seems so much lighter in weight and so much easier now. These last nine months have been awful — the death of Gracie's mum, the news about Gracie's dad and Julia, and then Gracie just going away for what, at first, seemed forever. And not only was she not there in-person, there was no talking or being in touch with each other for so long which was awful too. Now, Gracie is coming home and that can only be good stuff — and she wants us to meet up. Hooray times one million.

I could dance — so I did.

Nearly there

Those summer holidays were very strange. I was so happy to see Gracie again, but it was a different Gracie. It was as if she didn't want our friendship to be what it had been. She was distant but there. We just couldn't get as close and it would have been so easy to give up and find new friends, but that seemed wrong to both of us, so we carried on having nice, but awkward, times.

I talked to Mum. Isn't it odd that the person I planned to rebel against and still do rebel against at times is the one I turn to when things feel wrong — and Dad of course?

She said that Gracie had lost someone very important and perhaps she didn't want to get too close to me in case she got too close again, and then I was lost to her.

"She is protecting herself from more pain, I think," Mum said. "Just hang in there and see how it goes."

"But I lost too," I protested, "and she doesn't realise how unhappy and worried I have been."

Mum just looked at me sadly and walked away. I think she was telling me that what I lost I might be able to get back, but even if I couldn't get it back, it was no way the same as Gracie's loss.

Things got better slowly. I think we both accepted that things could never be as they were, but it could get better if we continued to try and wanted to try.

It was easier if I talked about the doings of my brothers and Potts the dog, and she was always interested in Grandad. Sometimes we talked about her mum and sometimes she got upset, but it wasn't difficult for either of us — and got easier. She talked a lot about all the things she did with the helpful lady at her school and how the activities always seemed easy, but they always helped her understand and feel what had happened.

Her dad's and Julia's wedding was coming close, and Julia took us to buy bridesmaid's dresses. Gracie and Julia get on very well — she called her Julia and will continue to call her Julia, even when she is her step-mum. We picked the same simple, mid-calf dress in different colours, and Julia thought we looked lovely.

I wonder if she would have said we looked grim if we had looked grim. Talking and being with Gracie is sometimes like hard work and it is easier to fib.

The wedding was lovely. It took place in the registry office and then we all had a meal in a posh restaurant. Mum and Dad, and the boys came along, and Julia's mother came from Cornwall. Grandad was also invited but he did not feel well enough and decided to have a quiet day with Potts. The boys behaved well enough. Gracie was quiet throughout but not unhappy and she was pleased when her dad talked about her mum, his other wife, as well as his new wife, in his speech.

He said that that he would always love his wife who had died but now there was room for someone else to love, and he was so happy that Julia was filling that new space. There are three spaces in his heart now, not two, and they are occupied by Gracie Pritchard, Mrs Pritchard number one, and Mrs Pritchard number two. He actually said it like this, as if he was emphasising that they were all Pritchards.

The new Mr and Mrs Pritchard went on honeymoon and Gracie stayed with us. She spent a lot of her time with Albie, who is the least awful of the twins. That felt okay and I wasn't jealous. We talked about whether her dad and Julia might have a baby and she straightaway said, "Oh, I hope so," and there was a little spark of real happiness.

Gracie also spent time with my mum who taught her to bake and cook. Gracie and I talked mainly when we were in bed — she had a blow-up mattress on the floor of my bedroom. We talked a lot then about what had happened. It seemed easier in the darkness. And Grandad was great. He played dominoes with her and said nothing. All she had to do was play dominoes — no pressure.

So, we have our friendship back — sort of. It will probably get easier when we are both back at school in the second year of secondary school, when there will be so much work to do there will be no time to think back.

As for my rebellion, well it rumbles on. I occasionally have huge shouting matches with Mum, and even Dad sometimes. They can both be so annoying and stupid sometimes. Sometimes I win and sometimes I lose.

I suppose I have had success since the rebellion began, in that my life is so much more sorted out by me now — not the big things but little things. I make a lot more decisions now and I think Mum and Dad trust me not to make daft decisions most of the time. But the biggest success was getting my best pal, Gracie Elizabeth Pritchard back. That means the most to me.

About the Author

Judith Humphries was born in Newcastle upon Tyne but her home has been in East Yorkshire for over forty years where she lives with her husband Steve. Judith has two children and two grandchildren. *The April Rebellion* is her first novel, and is an exciting and new direction after a long career in social work and lecturing.